Stephen & Lorna McConnell
"Lismaragh",
12 Red Fort Park,
Carrickfergus BT38 9EW
Tel: (09603) 68139

THE PARK PEOPLE

D0766477

To claire
with much love from

Jennifer Lewcombe

Thankyou for lending me
your mummy!

The Park People

JENNIFER REES LARCOMBE

KINGSWAY PUBLICATIONS
EASTBOURNE

First published 1992

Cover and text illustrations
by Sarah Hedley, Linda Rogers Associates

ISBN 0 85476 328 7

Printed in Great Britain for
Kingsway Publications Ltd
Lottbridge Drove, Eastbourne, E Sussex BN23 6NT by
Clays Ltd, St. Ives plc.
Typeset by J&L Composition Ltd, Filey, North Yorkshire

To my youngest son Richard
for all his help and advice

Contents

Chapter 1
Sam and the Nearly Unhappy
Birthday   9

Chapter 2
Graham and the Red Spots   27

Chapter 3
Kevin Who Needed a Friend   43

Chapter 4
Mark and Hetty the Horrible   59

Chapter 5
Matt and the Spook   75

Chapter 6
Darren—the King of the Park   89

CHAPTER ONE

Sam and the Nearly Unhappy Birthday

The park was like a big green field with a roundabout, swings and a slide. There were lots of flowers growing there and tall shady trees. A little lame man called Bert was the park-keeper—he weeded the flower-beds, swept the paths and always smiled at everyone. All the park people lived in little old houses round the edge of the park, and on one corner stood the church and on another the school.

Alice's house was very messy. That was probably because her mummy was an artist and painted pictures all day.

'She's far too busy to tidy up,' Alice told her friends in the park.

Sam lived next door to Alice, but

his house was always clean and tidy. The houses were so close together that from his bedroom window Sam could look right into Alice's bedroom.

'What a mess!' Sam's mum would say, but Sam thought it looked a lovely room. It was full of junk models Alice had made, pictures she had painted and toys, clothes and books she had left jumbled in happy heaps on the floor. Sam wished he had a room like that, but he didn't say so.

'You are never to go into that messy house,' said his mum.

If he squashed his nose against the glass of his bedroom window, Sam could see right down into Alice's kitchen. Alice and her mum and dad were always laughing and having fun together. Sometimes when he stood at his window in his pyjamas, Alice would wave goodnight to him before she drew her curtains. He

never waved back—his mum wouldn't like it.

Sam and his mum had not always lived in the old house by the park. Once he could remember having a garden and a daddy too.

'Will I still have to go to Mrs Baker's when I start school?' asked Sam as he ate his tea one day in their clean and tidy kitchen. Mrs Baker looked after Sam while his mum worked at the hairdresser's down the road. He did not like her very much. But he did not say so.

'Of course you'll still have to go to her after school,' said his mum crossly. 'I don't finish work until six, do I?'

'I could play in the park until you come home,' suggested Sam hopefully.

'What? Play with all those dirty, rough children?' exclaimed his mum in horror. Sam thought the children in the park looked very nice. But he didn't say so.

The day that Sam started school his mum scrubbed him so clean he felt he had no skin left. His new clothes felt stiff and funny as he walked across the park towards the school gate.

He quite liked his teacher, until she said, 'We're going to paint now, but we are not going to use brushes; we'll all use our fingers instead.'

Sam did not know what to do. His

mum never liked him to get his hands dirty. 'She'll be cross if I do,' he thought. But he did not say so. He sat down firmly on his clean hands and watched everyone else getting messy.

It was even worse in the playground. Everyone was rushing around making a noise and Sam had never rushed about and made a noise before. So he put his thumb in his mouth and stood on his own by the wall.

'Hello,' said a voice he recognised. 'You're the boy who never waves.' Alice was older than Sam but she had such a nice smily face he felt he could have liked her very much— if only she had not been so messy.

'Have some toffee,' said Alice, 'I made it myself. My mummy paints pictures and sells them,' she continued with her mouth full. 'I like painting too,' she added. Sam wondered if that was why they were both always covered in paint. But he did not say so.

'When my mum sees you looking out of your bedroom window she always says she'd like to paint a picture of you one day,' Alice went on. 'She says your face would look lovely in a frame.'

Sam thought a lot in bed that night, and an idea began to wriggle round in his head. Next day he found Alice in the playground and he said, 'If your mummy painted me, would she let me buy the picture? I've got 10p.'

It was his mum's birthday on Sunday. He could remember her last birthday when he and his daddy had gone out to buy her lots of presents and had wrapped them up in different coloured paper. This year he had been worried that she would not have any presents at all.

Alice smiled. 'I'm sure Mummy

would make a picture of you for 10p,' she said. 'If you come to our house tomorrow she'd do it in no time.'

Sam's mouth drooped sadly. 'I could never come to your house,' he said. 'So your mum won't be able to paint me after all.'

'Oh dear,' said Alice. 'Never mind, I'll talk to the park-keeper about that; he always knows what to do about everything.'

Sam couldn't imagine how that funny looking little man could possibly know what to do about anything. But he did not say so.

On the way home across the park Alice found Bert the park-keeper planting some new young trees by his shed. He was her very special friend because he was her Sunday school teacher at the church on the corner of the park. As usual he had a very good idea.

Next day Alice could hardly wait to find Sam. She was sparkling with excitement.

'Bert says why don't you look out of your window tonight so my mum can draw you from my bedroom? She says she'd love to.'

Sam was so pleased he smiled all the time he was having his picture done that evening. The smile came out beautifully in the painting.

'But how can I fetch it from your house?' he asked Alice next day in the playground.

Alice shut her eyes tight to help herself think. 'I know. I'll wrap it up in birthday paper and very early on your mum's birthday I'll hide it under your door mat.'

Sam smiled his biggest smile ever. 'I'll leave my 10p under the mat for her to find,' he thought. But he did not say so.

Early on Sunday morning Sam crept downstairs and opened the back door. His 10p was gone and a pretty parcel lay in its place. Quietly he crept into his mum's bedroom. She was sitting up in bed crying when he put his present down beside her. Sam thought she must be sad because she was not expecting any presents that day. But he didn't say so.

At first she looked very pleased with the picture. Then she said, 'Where did you get this?'

'Alice's mum next door paints pictures to sell and I gave her my 10p,' said Sam proudly.

'You never went into that messy house!' shouted his mum angrily.

'No,' said Sam. 'She painted me through the window.'

It was not a happy birthday. Mum did put the picture up on the wall of the sitting room, but she went on crying all day as she scrubbed and polished the clean little rooms. She always cleaned things when she was sad.

At tea time there was a knock on the door. It was Alice. She was holding a box she had decorated with all kinds of paper and ribbons. Inside were some honey biscuits she had just made. But Sam's mum still could not stop crying. Sam hoped her tears would not make the biscuits soggy. Then Alice's mummy came in with a birthday card in her hand. It was not a proper card, but a little picture of the park that she had painted herself. And Sam's mum cried even more. Suddenly Alice's mum put her arms all round Sam's mum and because no one had done that for so long Sam's mum rather liked it.

'We really came to ask you to tea in our kitchen,' said Alice. 'We've been making a birthday cake for you.'

Sam held his breath. It sounded such fun, but Mum would never say they could go. But he was wrong.

'All right,' she said unexpectedly. 'No one's made me a birthday cake for years.'

The cake was so good Sam ate three slices; then he and Alice worked on making junk models at the far end of the table while the mums drank tea and talked and talked. All about Sam's daddy who went away, and how hard it was working at the hairdresser's.

'But I have to pay the rent,' said Sam's mum. 'As well as paying Mrs Baker to look after Sam.'

'Why doesn't he come here after school?' said Alice. 'Mum wouldn't charge any money because he would keep me company.'

'Oh no!' said Sam's mum turning bright pink. 'Sam loves it at Mrs Baker's.'

Sam was just about to say nothing as usual, when instead he shouted, 'No I don't love it at Mrs Baker's! I hate going there!' He was painting a cereal box bright red and getting very messy doing so. 'It's too clean at Mrs Baker's,' he added more quietly. Suddenly Sam's mum was laughing for the first time for so long.

'It certainly isn't too clean here,' said Alice's mum, who was laughing too. 'We really would like to have him; Alice needs someone to play with.'

Soon it was all settled, and as they walked home Sam's mum said, 'I never knew such nice people lived round this park,' and her voice sounded all bubbly and different.

'Perhaps,' thought Sam, 'you can catch happiness from people as easily as you can catch a cold.'

But he didn't say so.

CHAPTER TWO

Graham and the Red Spots

In the house on the other side of Alice lived Graham. Alice did not like Graham very much.

'He's always so miserable,' she explained to the park-keeper. 'He's the most miserable boy I know. He's always grizzling about something. So I call him Grizzly Graham.'

'Why do you think he's so sad?' asked Bert as he pulled up the weeds.

'Well, he doesn't *have* to be sad,' replied Alice. 'He's got a nice mum and dad, a big sister and a rabbit as well. He only seems to notice horrid things and I've never seen him laugh—ever.'

'Well perhaps we ought to send up some "Secret Whispers" about him,' said Bert. Alice knew just what he meant. In Sunday school Bert was always telling his class that they could send Secret Whispers up to God any time they liked.

'But I don't want to do any Secret Whispers about Graham,' said Alice, ''cos I don't like him.'

'Perhaps you might like him if God made him happy,' suggested Bert, and he was smiling as he pushed his wheelbarrow away.

Alice was still looking doubtful when she got home. 'I hope God

hurries up and makes Grizzly Graham happy soon,' she told her mum. 'He's such a silly boy.'

'We could ask him to tea,' said her mum. 'He might like playing cars with Sam. That would cheer him up a bit. You can make some of your honey biscuits while I paint his picture.'

'Oh dear!' said Alice. 'I'd much rather let God make Graham happy without us having to help. We'll all have to put cotton wool in our ears if he comes here so his grizzling doesn't give us headaches.'

Graham felt rather pleased when they asked him to tea, but he managed to stop his face from showing it. He was very proud to have his picture painted by a real artist, but all he said was, 'I hope she won't take long to paint me; I hate sitting still.'

31

It was no fun at all having Grizzly Graham to tea. He would not eat fish fingers, and he did not like sausages, beefburgers or beans on toast. He would not play cars with Sam and he even said he hated honey biscuits.

The drawing only took a few minutes and then Alice took Graham to play in the park while her mum did the painting part—which took much longer. Even the park was no fun with Graham. He did not want to go on the slide or the swings. He wouldn't play ball or make a house in the bushes. In the end he fell over and grazed his knee.

'Come on home,' said Alice in a tired voice. 'I'll find you a plaster.'

'I've finished,' called Mum from her studio. 'I've done two pictures of you, Graham. Come and tell me which one you think is most like you.' Graham looked closely at the first

picture and saw a very miserable boy frowning back at him. He did not like the look of that boy very much. The second one was much nicer. It had a big, wide smile.

'This one's not a bit like me,' said Graham looking at the smiling boy.

'No,' said Mum. 'But don't you think you *could* look like that?'

'How can I?' grumbled Graham, and went home without even saying 'thank you'.

A week later, when Alice burst in from school with Sam, her mum met them in the hall.

'Poor Graham,' said Mum. 'He's really got something to be sad about now. His gran is very ill and so his mum has had to go to look after her.'

'But he's got a dad,' said Sam.

'Yes, but his dad's had to go away on business to Germany,' said Alice's mum. 'So I've asked Graham and his

sister to stay here with us for a bit.'
Alice was horrified.

'I like having Sam,' she said, 'but
I don't want Graham in my house.'

'I'm going to get paid for having
them,' said her mum. 'And that will
help when it's time for buying Christmas presents.'

'I wish we didn't have to keep on
helping God like this,' said Alice.
And she sounded almost as grizzly
as Graham himself.

The next day Graham and his sister
came. For the first week everyone
had to put up with Graham's grizzling
because, as Alice's dad pointed out,
'He's probably very homesick.'

After that, however, Mum just
could not stand it any longer. She
decided it was time to do something
about Graham.

'Graham,' she said, 'you haven't
had any pocket-money yet, have you?
Would you like some?'

Graham was pleased, but he tried not to let it show.

'We never actually give pocket-money in this family,' Mum continued. 'It has to be earned.'

'I'm not washing up,' grizzled Graham. But Alice's mum showed him a sheet of red shiny spots.

'I'm going to stick one of these on the calendar each day that I don't hear you grizzle once,' she said. 'And next Saturday every spot will have earned you 5p.'

'And I'll give you an extra red spot each time you laugh at something,' added Dad.

Graham may have been a very miserable person, but he was very good at doing sums in his head. His eyes began to gleam. 'I could earn 70p a week with those red spots!' he said, and he just could not help looking pleased this time.

'But you'll have to try very hard

36

to get them,' said Mum.

Graham did try—very hard indeed. He did not manage to laugh the next day, but he did not grizzle once, right up until bath-time.

'I don't need a bath!' he cried. 'I hate soap.'

Alice put her fingers in her ears and said, 'Bad luck, Graham. Bang goes your red spot for today.'

The next day was Monday, and something so funny happened that even Graham could not help laughing. He and his sister were walking to school with Sam and Alice when they met an old man. He wore a very old hat pulled down over his eyes and he was carrying a pair of gloves and a letter.

'I've quite forgotten where the post box is,' he said. 'Can you help me?'

'It's right behind you,' said Alice, trying not to giggle.

'Ah!' said the old man, and carefully posted his gloves and walked home with the letter still in his hand.

'Poor old man,' said Alice, running after him, but Graham laughed so much he had to roll about on the grass. He knew he was sure of a red spot that day.

Because laughing made him feel happy he never grizzled once for the rest of that day. But the next day he forgot and grizzled all the way across the park to school because it was so cold.

Just as they were about to go in through the school gate, Alice said, 'Look out, there's Hetty!'

Hetty was the ugliest, meanest dog in the park. She always chased people who were frightened of her. That morning she was chasing Mark, who was very frightened of her indeed. Mark knew the path leading

39

up to the school gate was covered in ice, but Hetty did not. Suddenly all four legs slipped from under her fat body and she span helplessly round and round in circles. Graham laughed so much he could hardly do his sums.

'You know what?' said Alice's dad a couple of weeks later. 'I can hardly wait for the train to bring me home from work these days so I can hear about all the funny things that keep happening round here.'

'I don't suppose Graham could grizzle now if he tried,' said Alice.

'I don't think I could,' laughed Graham. 'I seem to have forgotten how.'

It was the day Graham's mum was due to come home.

'Would you like to have one of the pictures I painted of you to take home?' asked Alice's mum. 'You look just like the smiling boy these days.'

40

'Ye-es,' said Graham slowly, 'but I think I'll take the miserable picture. If ever I feel like grizzling again, I'll only have to look at it to remember how horrid I was before.'

Alice smiled to herself. She knew her Secret Whispers had worked!

CHAPTER THREE

Kevin Who Needed a Friend

Kevin had the best bike in the park.

'And he's got two radio controlled cars as well!' thought Sam, though he did not say so. Sam, Alice and Graham were swinging in the after-tea sunshine watching Kevin practise wheelies and jumps.

'His dad gave him a stereo last week,' said a voice from high above their heads, 'and it wasn't even his birthday.' Matt always sat on top of the slide because he liked to be able to see everything that happened in the park. And he was also safe from Hetty up there. 'They say,' went on Matt, 'that Kevin's got a telly in every room of his house now.'

'What? Even in the bathroom?' laughed Graham.

'I wouldn't like to have Kevin's dad,' said Alice thoughtfully.

'Why?' asked Sam in surprise.

'That's why,' said Alice pointing. A train from the city had just rumbled into the station nearby and all the tired-looking people who had come home from work on it were walking across the park. Kevin's dad did not look tired at all. He hurried along ahead of them all in his black suit and shiny shoes. Children ran out of houses all round the park to hug their dads, but when Kevin whizzed up, his dad only nodded and walked on briskly, twirling his umbrella.

'He's too busy being important,' said Alice sadly. 'He only gives Kevin things to keep him quiet.'

'Kevin hasn't got any friends,' added Matt from the slide.

'If I had a bike like that, I wouldn't care if I didn't have any friends,' said Graham.

'Yes you would,' said Alice sternly. 'Everyone needs a friend.'

Two days later Alice came bursting into the studio where her mother was painting.

'Mum!' she shouted. 'You'll never guess what!'

'What won't I guess?' said her mum, smiling round the edge of her easel.

'The cross man from the sweet shop has gone, and a new family with two children are moving in today.'

47

'How lovely,' said Mum. 'Some brand new park people. What are they like?'

'There's a girl my sort of age. She's got lovely long black hair. And a big brother who looks very smiley. They come from India.'

'Why don't you make some of your honey biscuits as a welcome-to-the-park present?' said Mum, as she wiped her painty hands on her apron.

The new family were all standing behind the counter in the sweet shop, and they smiled when Alice and her mum gave them the honey biscuits.

'Will the children be going to Park School?' asked Mum. Suddenly the smiles disappeared from all their faces, and they looked worried.

'Yes,' said the father, 'and we hope they will be happy there.'

'I'm sure they will,' said Alice's

mum, but Alice was not so sure. She knew Darren. He was the biggest boy in the school and he always bullied new children.

'Why don't you come and meet some of my friends in the park now?' she suggested. 'Then you won't feel so shy when you get to school.'

'Everyone in my class will like you,' she told Savita, as they twirled on the roundabout. 'But if Raj is in Year Seven, he'll have to put up with Darren and his gang.'

Kevin was riding round them on just the back wheel of his bike.

'This is Raj and Savita,' said Alice, but Kevin did not say hello. He never talked to any of the park people. He went to a different school on the other side of town.

'No wonder he's got no friends,' said Alice with a sigh. It was just then that Darren came towards them.

'What are you two doing here?' demanded Darren, glaring at Savita and Raj. 'This is our park. We don't like strangers here. Go away or I'll punch you.'

'My sister and I will not go away,' replied Raj quietly, so Darren punched him.

'A fight! A fight!' shouted Darren's gang, and even Hetty the dog ran up barking fiercely.

'Darren is bigger than anyone else,' Alice explained to her mum later. 'He's always being mean. His gang would have hurt Raj badly if the park-keeper hadn't come just then. He's always there when we need him.'

When Sam and Alice arrived home from school the next day, Mum asked, 'How did Savita and Raj get on today?'

'Savita was happy,' replied Alice,

'but poor Raj was all alone in the playground. I'm going to send up some Secret Whispers about him. Everyone needs a friend.'

The next evening Matt was sitting at the top of the slide as usual. Alice, Sam and Graham were on the swings.

'Something's wrong with Kevin's dad,' said Matt from his high-up seat. Across the park came all the tired train people but that day Kevin's dad was trailing along behind them all.

'He looks like a popped balloon,' said Alice.

Kevin's dad certainly looked very odd.

'P'raps he's got tummy-ache,' said Sam.

'Has your dad got tummy-ache?' Matt asked Kevin the next evening. 'He never went to work on the train today.'

52

'Of course he hasn't got tummy-ache!' snapped Kevin. 'He's lost his job, but he'll soon get a better one.' He was always boasting. But Kevin's dad did not get another job. Soon Kevin's bike began to look shabby and he grew out of his smart new clothes. A 'For Sale' notice was put up outside his house and one of the cars disappeared from the garage.

'Kevin's mum's gone for good,' said Matt from the top of the slide one day. 'I saw her drive off with millions of cases and her cat.'

The next morning something very strange happened. Instead of Kevin driving off to his school on the far side of town he walked towards Park School with everyone else.

Darren and his gang were standing at the school gate. 'What are you doing here, Kevin?' they demanded.

'My school got burned down,' said Kevin airily. Everyone knew he was making that up. They knew he had to change schools because his dad had lost his job.

'We don't want your sort here,' said Darren in first play.

'This is a horrid school anyway,' said Kevin as he went off to stand on his own by the wall.

'It would be a good school without Darren,' said Raj, who was also standing alone nearby. 'Have some of my sweets.'

A few months later Alice was talking to the park-keeper. She liked watching him plant flowers in straight neat rows. 'Kevin and Raj have been friends ever since,' she was telling him. 'I sent up some Secret Whispers because they both needed a friend. But wasn't it clever of God to make them friends with each other?'

They were both so busy talking that Kevin had walked right up to them before they noticed him. He looked as if he wanted to cry.

'Darren and his lot have broken my bike,' he said. 'Do you think you could mend it?'

Bert was always mending things for the Park People. He may have looked a bit funny, but everyone loved him.

'Has your dad got a job yet?' asked Bert kindly, as he worked on the broken bike at the door of his shed.

'No,' said Kevin sadly. 'He thinks he'll never get one now, so he just sits all alone in the kitchen all day long.'

'We'd better do some Secret Whispers for Kevin's dad to get a friend too,' said Alice when Kevin had ridden away.

It was the very next day when Kevin burst into his kitchen with Raj close behind him. Kevin's dad was sitting with his feet up on the kitchen table. He hadn't washed up anything for days.

'Dad!' shouted Kevin. 'Something dreadful has happened.'

'What?' growled his father.

'Raj's dad was painting their shop window, when he fell off the ladder and hurt his back.'

'So?' said Kevin's dad crossly.

'So ... so there's no one to run the sweet shop while he's in hospital,' said Kevin impatiently.

'What about his wife?' said Kevin's dad even more crossly.

'My mother would indeed be happy to do it,' said Raj. 'But soon she has a new baby and the doctor says she must keep up her feet.'

'Listen, Dad,' said Kevin excitedly. 'You're so clever at business, why don't you run the shop? Raj and I will help you after school and at weekends.'

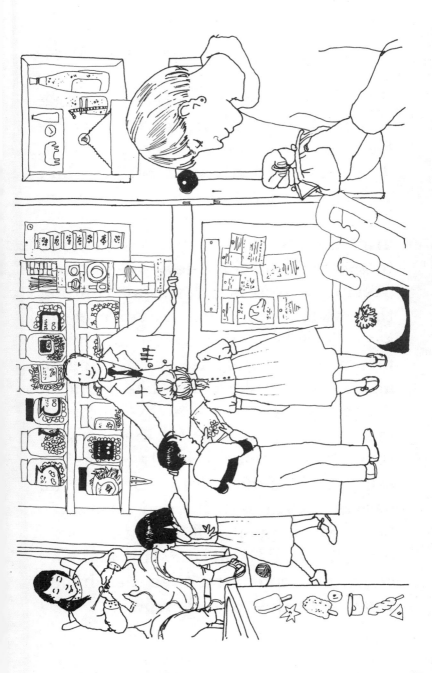

'Me! Run a tiny little sweet shop?' yawned his dad.

'It would be fun, Dad,' pleaded Kevin. Suddenly his dad took his feet off the kitchen table and said, 'I suppose anything's better than sitting here all day.'

'And do you know what?' said Alice to the park-keeper a few weeks later. 'Kevin's dad is so clever at running that sweet shop that Savita's mum says it has never made so much money before. But the best thing of all is that Kevin's dad has found a friend too. He goes every night to see Raj's dad in hospital. Savita says they keep making lovely plans to sell lots of other things as well as sweets. Kevin says his dad has never been so happy in all his life.'

'Well, well,' said Bert, and he smiled a secret smile as he limped away with his wheelbarrow.

CHAPTER FOUR

Mark and Hetty the Horrible

Hetty was not a nice dog. Her tail was so short she could not have wagged it even if she had wanted to. She only chased people who were frightened of her and Mark was very frightened of her indeed. Every time he crept nervously into the park Hetty appeared from nowhere, barking madly and showing her horrid yellow teeth.

'Silly little boy!' said Hetty's owner, Miss Lee. 'She wouldn't hurt a fly.' But Mark did not believe her.

Hetty and Miss Lee looked just alike. They were both fat, with yellow teeth and small, mean eyes. Whatever the children did in the park, Miss Lee was cross about it.

'Stop making so much noise!' she would shout. 'Don't ride your bikes so fast.' 'You shouldn't play football, you'll spoil the grass.'

'The park-keeper doesn't mind,' Graham told her.

'The park-keeper!' snorted Miss Lee. 'Every week I complain to the Town Hall about him. He ought to keep you children in order instead of mending your toys and sticking plasters on your knees.'

'But he works very hard to make the park look pretty,' said Alice almost in tears. Everyone loved Bert —except Miss Lee and Hetty.

'I'll make them get rid of him,' she growled, sounding just like her nasty dog.

'Oh dear,' thought Alice who was really crying by now. 'I'll have to send up some very big Secret Whispers about this.'

'We must get rid of Miss Lee,' said Kevin, 'before she gets rid of Bert.' And just for once everyone agreed with him. 'I've got a catapult,' he added. 'I could "ping" her with a stone every time she comes into the park.'

'And I could sit up here on the slide and pour buckets of water on top of her head,' suggested Matt.

'What are you planning?' smiled Bert as he passed by on his way to the shed.

'We've got to get rid of a terrible enemy,' said Alice. 'Before she gets rid of you.'

'You mean Miss Lee,' laughed Bert.

'Yes, she's always getting me into trouble with my boss at the Town Hall. But I take no notice. Do you want to know how to get rid of an enemy?' he added.

'Yes!' they all said as they clustered closely round him.

'The best way is to be so kind to them that they turn into a friend.'

'I'd rather use my catapult,' said Kevin.

'Maybe you would,' laughed the little park-keeper. 'But Miss Lee might catch you and call the police. Then she'd have won, wouldn't she?'

The next day Sam picked a huge bunch of the park-keeper's best flowers and gave them to Miss Lee. She was very pleased, but Bert was not. However, he knew why Sam had done it, so he was not cross.

Matt weeded Miss Lee's garden for her, and Raj and Kevin took her a large bag of pear drops from the

sweet shop. Alice even gave Hetty some of her home-made toffee, but it glued up the dog's yellow teeth so she couldn't bark for hours.

In fact everyone was so nice to Miss Lee that she wrote to her sister up north and said, 'I used to think children nowadays had no manners but now I am changing my ideas.'

One day Mark was walking across the park on his way to tea with Alice. He loved it at Alice's house but he was so scared of Hetty that he hated to cross the park to get there. As he walked along he kept looking nervously over his shoulder and his heart went bump bump bump. 'Wherever can she be today?' he wondered, as he rang the bell on Alice's front door.

'Let's creep up to the studio and give Mum a surprise,' said Alice.

As they peeped through the crack in the studio door, Mark saw a

66

dreadful sight. There on a high stool sat Hetty, like an ugly fat fairy on top of a Christmas tree. She was having her portrait painted. Mark shrank back into the darkness of the passage but it was too late, Hetty had sniffed him. She leapt off her high stool and barking furiously she jumped up on Mark, pinning him to the wall as she showed her nasty yellow teeth.

'Silly boy,' said Miss Lee. 'She wouldn't hurt a fly.'

'It was my idea,' whispered Alice to Mark, as Hetty was lifted back onto her stool. 'I thought Miss Lee would like a picture of Hetty, but Mum says it's going to be the ugliest picture she's ever painted!'

Miss Lee however was so pleased with it when it was finished she actually gave Alice a kiss.

'Mark,' said his dad the following

Saturday. 'Go out and play in the park. I want some peace to read my paper.' Mark's dad was a huge policeman and he wasn't frightened of anything so Mark could not explain about Hetty. Dad would never have understood. Out he had to go while his knees knocked together in fright and his eyes darted this way and that—watching for Hetty. When at last he saw her, he sighed with relief—she was safely tied up in her garden. He was having a lovely peaceful swing when he saw Miss Lee struggling across the park carrying two very heavy shopping bags.

'I suppose I ought to help her,' he sighed and he began to run towards Miss Lee. Hetty however had also seen Miss Lee, and in no time she had broken the string which was tied to her collar. Over the garden fence she jumped and bounded across the grass. Mark panicked. He did not

look where he was running and—
bang! He shot right into Miss Lee
like a cannon ball.

She sat down hard on the ground
and everything inside her shopping
bags fell out all over the path. Eggs
cracked, bottles broke and apples
rolled away into the mud. Mark
stood looking down in horror while
Miss Lee and Hetty glared up at
him with their small mean eyes.

'How many more times must I tell
you? She wouldn't hurt a fly!' barked
Miss Lee.

'Oh dear, oh dear!' said the park-
keeper, running out of his shed. 'Let
me help you home, Miss Lee, and
make you a nice cup of tea. Then
Mark and I'll pop and buy more of
the things that were spoiled when
you fell.'

'I haven't any more money,' said
Miss Lee crossly. 'I've been saving
from my pension for weeks for this

shopping. My sister from the north is coming to stay with me today and I wanted to feed her really well. I'll make this silly boy's father pay for all the damage.' Mark gasped. He could easily guess what his father would do.

'You know, it wasn't really the lad's fault, was it?' said Bert patting Miss Lee's hand kindly. 'You let me have your shopping list, and I'll buy those things for you. I don't have much to spend my money on, not having a family of my own.'

When Bert and Mark walked back across the park an hour later, they were carrying five large shopping bags instead of two and they were full of all kinds of special treats. After that Miss Lee never wrote to the Town Hall to complain about Bert again.

Early next morning Mark's dad sent him to buy a Sunday paper at the sweet shop. Poor Mark was so frightened he might meet Hetty he could hardly breathe.

As soon as she saw him, Hetty leapt over her garden fence all ready for the chase. It was Alice's ginger cat who saved Mark. She was taking a morning stroll across the park and she was just as frightened of Hetty as Mark was. Up the steps of the slide she darted with Hetty close behind. She did not think Hetty would dare to follow her up there, but she was wrong. As Hetty scrambled up the steps the cat slid down the slide to safety leaving the dog barking madly on the platform high above.

Hetty was far too frightened to go down the steps or the slide, and she froze into a quivering heap of terror. Mark looked desperately round the park. It was too early for anyone to be about and if he ran for help

Hetty might fall down and be badly hurt. There was only one thing to do, and Mark did the bravest thing he had ever done. He climbed the steps—lifted Hetty into his arms and slid down the slide with her on his lap.

Now Hetty had a very good memory and she never forgot someone who was kind to her. So from that day she never barked at Mark or chased him again.

In fact they became quite friendly, and when Mark appeared in the park Hetty's stump of a tail would start to wag, and she showed her yellow teeth—not in a snarl, but in a wide friendly grin.

CHAPTER FIVE

Matt and the Spook

Everyone who lived round the park called him Old Hat, because he was a very old man and his hat was even older than he was.

'He's silly,' thought Matt from his seat at the top of the slide. 'How dumb to read a book while he's walking along. One day he'll trip over and hurt himself.'

Old Hat really did seem to spend most of his time wandering round the park with his head in a book. Every time Graham saw him he had to laugh because he was remembering the time the old man had posted his gloves and walked home with the letter still in his hand!

Matt did not laugh, because he didn't like people who read books. He had tried very hard to learn to read when he first went to school, but the teacher kept on saying, 'You never *try*, Matt.' So of course he had stopped trying and just given up. Now all his class were off the reading scheme and on to library books, but Matt was stuck fast on Red Book Three and he and his teacher were sick of it.

'Hello Dumbo!' shouted Darren as he and his gang walked past the slide. They were off to play football in the far corner of the park. They never asked Matt to play because he always fell over his boots and never saw the ball coming until it hit him. Everyone at school called Matt 'Dumbo', because he could not read and no one ever wanted to play with him. So he just sat at the top of the slide and soon he knew everything about everyone who lived round the park.

One afternoon however, Matt saw something that startled him so much he nearly fell down. It was a very high slide and from the top Matt could see clearly into the upstairs windows of the houses nearby.

'That's a spook!' gasped Matt in terror. 'And it's flapping about in Old Hat's bedroom.'

He tumbled quickly down the slide. When he reached the ground he could not see the terrifying white thing waving round any more, so he felt a bit braver. As he crept towards

79

Old Hat's front door and put his ear to the letter box, his face turned green again with fright. He could hear a horrid moaning groaning noise and he ran faster than he'd ever run in his life before.

Bang! He crashed right into the park-keeper and because he was very big for his age, and the park-keeper was very small for his, they both landed in a heap. Bert was not like other park-keepers so he was not cross.

'You look as if you've seen a ghost, young Matthew,' he said, brushing mud from his trousers.

'I have!' squeaked Matt. 'But you can only see it from the top of the slide. Please come and see.'

'I haven't climbed up here for years,' puffed the little park-keeper as he pulled himself up the steps.

'Can you see it?' demanded Matt from the ground below.

'It looks more like a flag than a spook,' said Bert.

'It couldn't be a flag,' said Matt crossly. 'No one's there to wave it.'

'We'd better go and get my ladder,' said Bert. 'But seeing I'm up here I'll just . . .' and he actually slid all the way down the slide—as if he were a little boy again. 'I haven't done that for years either,' he said happily.

Soon Bert fetched his ladder from the shed. 'You hold it tight,' he said as he put it up against Old Hat's house and began to climb. Matt was so scared he shut his eyes and held his breath. He did not want to see that spook ever again.

'Are you all right in there, Sir?' called Bert, knocking on the window. But all they could hear was a groan.

'I'm going to pull this window open a bit more, young Matt,' said Bert.

'Then you can squeeze through and let me in the front door.'

'Oh no!' gasped Matt. 'I'm not going in there. I'm not nearly brave enough.'

'God can make us brave when we have to be,' replied the park-keeper. 'I think the poor old man has fallen down and hurt himself.'

Poor Matt was shaking like an earthquake but he managed to scramble through the window, and there on the floor on the far side of the bed lay Old Hat. He was still wearing his hat, but just for once he was not reading a book.

'I tripped over last night,' he whispered. 'I think my leg is broken.' He had tied a pillow case to his walking stick and that was what Matt had thought was a spook.

'Fancy being frightened of a pillow case,' thought Matt as he opened the front door for Bert.

The ambulance made such a loud noise that all the park people looked out of their houses, and Matt, who loved telling news, felt more important than he ever had in his life.

Several weeks later Matt was sitting on the slide when he saw his spook again. He wasn't scared at all this time, because he could see Old Hat sitting up in his bed waving the pillow case.

'He must be home from hospital,' thought Matt. 'And I think he wants to see me.'

'The key's under the pot of geraniums,' shouted the old man when he heard Matt fumbling at the door.

'I just wanted to say thank you,' said Old Hat, when Matt had fought his way through the piles of books to reach the bed. 'I might have died of cold if you had not seen my signal. I would like to give

84

you a present. How about a nice book?'

'Oh no, thank you!' said Matt in horror. 'I hate books ... I can't read.'

'A football then?'

'I can't kick either,' said Matt gloomily. 'I can't do anything much.'

'I love books,' said Old Hat.

'I can see that!' replied Matt. 'You must have millions of them here— it's worse than a library.'

'Come on,' said Old Hat, 'there must be something you like.'

'Well, I like boats,' said Matt. 'When I grow up, I'm going to sail away in one and never ever come back.'

'I love boats too,' said Old Hat. 'I've got some wonderful pictures of boats in my books. Reach some down from that shelf and we'll enjoy ourselves.'

That night Matt was late home for tea for the first time ever!

Soon he was spending all his spare time with Old Hat and as they worked their way through his boat books he found the old man was teaching him to read without Matt really noticing it.

'I've spent all my life teaching people to read,' said Old Hat. 'And I can't think why your friends call you Dumbo. You are really a very clever boy.'

Soon Matt was reading and writing really well, but he never told his teacher because he did not like her. So he was still stuck on Red Book Three.

'Dumbo,' said Darren one day, in the playground. 'Mr Sweep wants to see you.'

Matt was almost as frightened of the headmaster as he was of spooks, but he remembered God could make him brave as he knocked on the office door.

'I've been wondering if this is really the right school for you, Matthew,' began Mr Sweep. Matt was horrified. He did not want to go to a new school.

'But,' continued Mr Sweep, 'I've heard from Mr Turner that you can read and write very well indeed.'

'Who's Mr Turner?' asked Matt blankly. Then he guessed. That must be Old Hat's proper name.

Mr Sweep pushed Red Book Three

across his desk, and Matt read it perfectly, and Red Books Six and Ten. When he had finished Mr Sweep said, 'You do realise your friend Mr Turner wrote Red Book Three and all the other reading books we use in this school?' And Matt's mouth fell open in amazement.

'Fancy Old Hat being that clever!' he thought.

'Dumbo!' jeered Darren, when Matt walked back into the playground again.

'I'm not a Dumbo any more,' said Matt coolly, and walked on by with his head held high.

Being able to read made Matt feel so good inside he even found he could play football better, and later on, when he was picked for the school team, he did not have much time for sitting on top of the slide any more.

CHAPTER SIX

Darren—the King of the Park

When Darren's dad went to prison his mum sat down by the telly and didn't seem to care much about anything any more. Darren didn't mind—he was King of the Park. Everyone was frightened of him and little children ran home when he came out to play. He was the biggest boy in Park School, and even Mr Sweep the headmaster was rather nervous of Darren. But there was one person who was not afraid of Darren, and that was Bert. 'But he ought to be,' thought Darren. "Cos I'm bigger than he is.'

It was the first day of the autumn half-term week, and Darren and his gang were holding a meeting in their hide-out in the corner of the churchyard.

'We're going to teach that park-keeper a lesson,' said Darren.

It was the busiest time of the year for Bert. He had to rake up all the leaves into piles and then barrow them away to the compost heap behind his shed. But every time his back was turned Darren and his gang jumped out of hiding, and kicked the piles of leaves into the air, so the wind could scatter them all over the grass again. They watched to see him getting cross, but the park-keeper just raked up the leaves and never said a word.

'Look, Darren's lot are laughing at him again,' said Alice angrily as she and her friends watched the park-keeper limping towards his shed. Behind him Darren and his gang were all walking with a limp, copying the funny way he waddled along.

'He knows they're laughing at him, but he's still smiling,' thought Sam but he did not say so. As they watched, Bert began to hop and jump about and wave his arms in the air. Then he looked over his shoulder to see if the gang would do that too.

'So you want to play "follow my leader", do you?' said Bert. The gang stopped and began to turn very red. They slunk away to their hide-out while everyone else began to laugh.

'We'll do him for that!' muttered

Darren. After they had added up all their money they went off to buy some white spray paint.

'The park-keeper is a silly old fool,' Darren wrote all along the side of the shed. Later when he came back to see if Bert was trying to scrub it off, he found this written underneath: 'I know that, Darren. Love from Bert.'

Darren was so cross he used up all his paint on the old man's wheel-barrow.

Next morning all the newly-planted wall flowers had been ripped out of the flower beds and stamped on, and the bark of all the new little trees had been stripped off with a sharp penknife.

'They'll die without their bark, won't they?' said Alice indignantly as she stood beside Bert who was sadly shaking his head.

'Why don't you go and tell Mark's

dad about Darren? He's a policeman.'

'I'm sending up some Secret Whispers about him first,' replied Bert. 'God will show me what to do about Darren when the right time comes.'

It was rather a special week in the park, because the church was holding a holiday club. Bert wanted to help so much, but he was too busy sweeping up the leaves to take the time off.

'Fancy going to church every day of the holidays,' sneered Darren.

'But they have prizes at the end of the week,' said one of his gang wistfully.

'And squash and cakes every day,' added another. The next morning they went to holiday club too, and Darren was left all alone. There weren't even any little children to frighten—they had all gone as well.

'You'll never guess what Darren's done now!' said Alice to Bert that afternoon. 'We were having such a lovely story at holiday club but Darren kept throwing mud bombs at the windows so we couldn't listen and when a teacher went out to stop him he threw one right in her eye. If I was God,' she added crossly, 'I'd throw such a big mud pie at Darren, it would squash him flat.'

'But God would never do that,' smiled the park-keeper. 'Because he loves Darren just as much as he loves you.'

'Does he?' said Alice in amazement.

On Saturday the park-keeper was asked to give out the holiday club prizes, and when Darren saw him disappearing into church he had an idea. The shed stood on six stone blocks, so it was easy to push some dry leaves and newspaper underneath it and then light a match.

Darren never really meant to burn the shed right down, but he had

forgotten that the park-keeper stored the petrol for his lawnmower inside. Suddenly there was a huge bang and flames leapt from the shed.

Darren sprang for cover behind the compost heap as the park-keeper and the vicar rushed out of church.

'There's something in there I must rescue,' gasped Bert, unlocking the shed door.

'You can't go in there!' yelled the vicar, but he was too late.

'Call a fire engine!' shouted a Sunday school teacher.

'And the ambulance,' added the vicar grimly.

When Bert ran out of his shed the sleeve of his coat was on fire, and if the vicar had not wrapped his own jacket round him and smothered the flames he might have been badly burned. But the park-keeper was carrying something safely wrapped in an old sack and when he drove off in the ambulance he was smiling happily.

The next day was Sunday, and Darren was disgusted to see all his gang going to church with the other park people.

'We're not playing with you any more, Darren,' they said. 'Fancy burning down the park-keeper's shed—he never did us any harm.'

When the door closed behind them all, Darren felt very lonely but he went off to make the biggest mud bomb he could throw. Just as he was about to hurl it at the church window a voice behind him spoke.

'Oh no you don't, young Darren.' And there stood Bert with one arm in a sling. 'You can burn down my shed, pull up my flowers and kill my baby trees, but I'm not going to let you throw one more lump of mud at God's house.' Darren dropped the bomb guiltily. There did not seem much point in running away—he felt more like crying really.

'Your dad wouldn't like you to land up in prison with him, would he?' said Bert kindly.

'He wouldn't care,' said Darren. 'No one minds what happens to me.'

'I used to feel just like that too, once,' said Bert. 'I was far worse than you when I was your age. See that ugly old house over there? That used to be an orphanage and I lived there when my mum died. I was the naughtiest boy in Park School then. In those days we were made to go to Sunday school each week and I was so bad I spoiled every story my old teacher told us. But one day she gave me a present.' From his pocket Bert produced a battered old Bible. 'In the front she wrote, "Don't ever forget that God loves you." That gave me such a shock it changed my life. I kept this Bible in my shed, and that's how I got my arm burned—running in to rescue it yesterday. I've got a present for you too, Darren,' he added, fumbling in his other pocket.

'For me?' gasped Darren. It was another Bible, but this one was new.

'I've written the same thing inside yours,' said Bert. '"Don't ever forget that God loves you."'

'Come on—he doesn't really ... does he?' gulped Darren.

'Course he does and don't you forget it!'

'I won't—ever,' said Darren in a wobbly little voice. 'And I'll look after this present all my life, even if I get both arms burned doing it.'

When all the park people came out of church they saw Darren sitting on the parkbench while Bert told him stories of some of the naughty things he had done when

he was King of the Park.

'Well!' said Alice in amazement. 'Just look what Secret Whispers have done now!'

The Curse Of Craigiburn

by Jennifer Rees Larcombe

They said that Craigiburn was cursed. The curtains were always drawn, and it was a sad family that lived in it.

James Brodie lived there now, with his father. What was the curse? Why would no one tell him? And why did the Ugly Man of the Forest send him away when he found out who he was?

Jamie was determined to find the answer to his questions. Little did he know how events would conspire to help him, especially once an old book came back from the distant past.

Phoenix

Published by Kingsway

Tracy And The Warriors

by Lynda Neilands

Tracy is a nine-year-old Brownie, and she is homesick. Sent to stay with her grim aunt and her wild cousin, she pours out all her woes in letters to God.

Her cousin and his friends (a gang of so-called warriors) lose no time in making life difficult for Tracy, but she finds help from the visiting Circus. When the warriors burn down Carlo the clown's caravan, all seems lost. Is it possible for anything good to come out of such a disaster?

LYNDA NEILANDS is the writer of *The Brownie Handbook*. She lives with her family in Dublin, in the Republic of Ireland.

Kingsway Publications

Jessica Joins The Brownies

by Lynda Neilands

Bullied at school, neglected at home, Jessica longs to have friends and be invited to parties like everyone else.

Mrs Lovett, the Guider, believes that Brownies are the answer. She makes it sound so easy. As if Jessica can simply show up at the hall and join in.

But nothing is simple when you have a grandmother and a brother who, like Cinderella's ugly sisters, seem bent on ruining your chance of happiness.

After the first few meetings Jessica is almost in despair. Until she discovers what being a Brownie and doing her duty to God is *really* about...

LYNDA NEILANDS lives in Northern Ireland with her husband and twin sons. She writes regularly for the Girl Guides Association and for Scripture Union.

Also from Kingsway by the same author, *Tracy And The Warriors*.

Kingsway Publications

While Others Dance

by Barbara Beacham

What do you do when the thing you most want and pray for can't be yours?

More than anything, Roslin longs to be a ballet dancer. What she can't understand is why her guardian Aunt Sarah is so determined to stop her dancing.

Suddenly Aunt Sarah has to move overseas, and Roslin finds herself at boarding school. Even there, it seems, there is a conspiracy against her dancing. Ballet is not taught at the school, and one of the other girls—a talented dancer herself—seems set on making Roslin's life unhappy.

Why will no one let her dance? Is Roslin destined to sit off-stage for ever, while others dance?

Barbara Beacham is the well-loved author of many children's books including *Island of Grey Mist*.

Published by Kingsway